The Fool
and the Fish

First published in the United States by Dial Books
A Division of Penguin Books USA Inc.
375 Hudson Street
New York, New York 10014
Published simultaneously in Canada
by Fitzhenry & Whiteside Limited, Toronto

Published in Austria as *Der Hecht hat's gesagt!*
by Esslinger im OBV, Vienna
Text copyright © 1990 by Dial Books
Illustrations copyright © 1990 by Verlag J.F. Schreiber,
Esslingen, West Germany
All rights reserved
Printed in Belgium
Typography by Robert Olsson
First American Edition
E
1 3 5 7 9 10 8 6 4 2

Library of Congress Cataloging in Publication Data
Hort, Lenny. The fool and the fish.
Based on Russian folk tale Po shchuch'emu velen'iu.
Summary: A retelling of the traditional Russian tale in
which a lazy fool catches an enchanted fish which promises
him that every wish he ever makes will come true.
1. Folklore—Soviet Union
I. Afanasyev, A. N. (Alexander Nikolayevich), 1826–1871.
II. Spirin, Gennady., ill.
III. Po shchuch'emu velen'iu. IV. Title.
PZ8.1.H8618Fo 1990 398.21'0947   89-26013
ISBN 0-8037-0861-0

Gennady Spirin

The Fool
and the Fish

A tale from Russia
by Alexander Nikolayevich Afanasyev
Retold by Lenny Hort

DIAL BOOKS  NEW YORK

Once there were three brothers. Yasha and Sasha were hardworking and clever, and so were their wives, Masha and Dasha. But Ivan was too lazy to get married. As long as he could lie around on top of the fireplace all day, he didn't care if everybody called him a fool.

One day Yasha and Sasha set out for market. "Give our wives a hand, and we'll bring you back a fine red robe and hat and boots."

"Green boots!" said Ivan.

Soon Masha and Dasha asked him to fetch some water. Ivan just yawned. "We'll tell your brothers, Fool," they said, "and you can forget about the new boots."

With a weary sigh the Fool took a couple of pails and dipped them in the icy stream. But when he drew one out, he found a king-size fish, the most handsome pike he had ever seen, splashing around inside. "Fish soup!" the Fool howled with joy.

"Don't be a fool," the pike spoke aloud. "Throw me back, and every wish you ever make will come true."

"Only a fool would listen to a talking fish," said Ivan, but he threw the pike back in the water. Before it swam away, the Fool called after it, *Fish, fish, fish! Grant my wish: Make those buckets of water carry themselves home.* And the buckets flew right through the snow, with Ivan chasing along behind them.

Fish, fish, fish! Grant my wish:

Just as he was settling back down over the fireplace, Masha and Dasha asked him to go to the forest and fetch some wood. Ivan just sucked his thumb. "We'll tell your brothers, Fool," they said.

With a weary sigh he shuffled over to the sleigh. Just as he was groaning at the thought of hitching up the horses, he remembered the pike and sang aloud, *Fish, fish, fish! Grant my wish: Take me to the woods!* And with Ivan on board, the sleigh raced across town, knocking over everything and everyone in its path.

It came to a stop in the forest. Ivan lay back comfortably and said, *Fish, fish, fish! Grant my wish: Make the ax and the saw do all the work!* In minutes invisible hands had chopped down tall trees, split them into logs, and loaded them up on the sled. Then the Fool climbed on top and wished himself headed for home.

The sleigh sped across town, scattering chickens and turning over market stalls. An angry mob finally caught up with the Fool and tried to drag him away. But Ivan cried out, *Fish, fish, fish! Grant my wish: Beat them off!* All at once heavy sticks rose up from the sleigh and pummeled the crowd till they all took to their heels.

The townspeople begged the Tsar to arrest the Fool.
So royal messengers visited Ivan's fireplace and asked him to
come with them to the palace. Ivan just scratched his nose.
"The Tsar will give you a fine red robe and hat and boots,"
they said.

"Green boots!" said Ivan.

"As you wish," said the Tsar's men.

And Ivan said, *Fish, fish, fish! Grant my wish: Take me to the palace!* Instantly Ivan was racing across town, fireplace and chimney and all. This time everybody dodged out of his way.

The palace was in an uproar when the flying fireplace came to a stop right in the throne room. All eyes turned to the Fool. "Why have you been making so much trouble?" demanded the Tsar.

"Why won't everyone just let me sleep," yawned the Fool. The Tsar's daughter had never seen anyone behave so boldly to her father. Her eyes met the Fool's, and all at once the two of them were madly in love. The Princess begged the Tsar to marry her to the dashing young stranger.

Fish, fish, fish! Grant my wish:

The furious Tsar ordered the Fool and the Princess married at once, then had the two of them sealed in a barrel and thrown upon the open sea.

Ivan did not resist. He was so happy to be alone with his bride that he had nothing else to wish for. But after a night of tossing on the waves, the Princess began to get hungry and seasick. "My darling, do something," she said.

That was all the urging Ivan needed: *Fish, fish, fish! Grant my wish: Land us safe on shore.*

The barrel shot right through the water and popped open on a lonely beach. "Oh, Ivan," said the Princess, "where will we live?"

The Fool took her in his arms and said, *Fish, fish, fish! Grant my wish: Give us a palace to rival the Tsar's, and set it down under his window.* It was just after dawn when they went inside their new home and lay down on a bed even more comfortable than Ivan's old spot on the fireplace.

When the Tsar saw the enchanted palace he decided he'd rather have the Fool for a son-in-law than for an enemy. He brought Ivan a new robe and hat and boots—green boots— and they begged each other's forgiveness. The whole country celebrated the wedding with vodka and fish soup, and they all lived in peace.

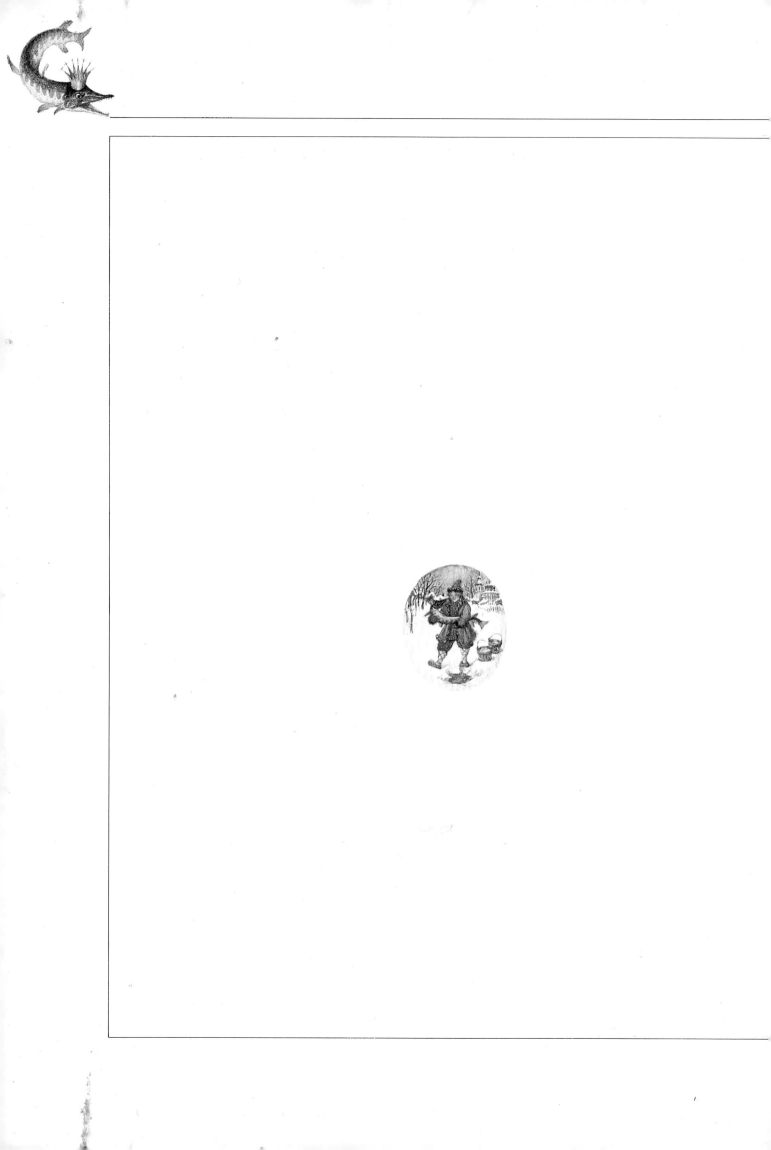